For Pop Read, who sat me on his lap when I was three
and showed me how to draw a sparrow – J.C.

Seven for a Secret copyright © Frances Lincoln Limited 2006
Text copyright © Laurence Anholt 2006
Illustrations copyright © Jim Coplestone 2006

The right of Laurence Anholt to be identified as the Author of this work
has been asserted by him in accordance with the Copyright, Designs and Patents Act, 1988.

This edition published in Great Britain in 2006 by
Frances Lincoln Children's Books, 4 Torriano Mews,
Torriano Avenue, London NW5 2RZ

www.franceslincoln.com

Distributed in the USA by Publishers Group West

A version of this story was first published under the title **The Magpie Song**
in 1995 by Egmont Children's Books.

British Library Cataloguing in Publication Data available on request

ISBN 1-84507-300-2

Printed in Singapore

1 3 5 7 9 8 6 4 2

Visit the Anholt website at www.anholt.co.uk

Seven
for a
Secret

Laurence Anholt
Illustrated by Jim Coplestone

FRANCES LINCOLN CHILDREN'S BOOKS

Dear Grampa,

It's noisy in the city and I can't sleep.
I hear police cars, a dog barking and the TV next door.
I see a million orange lights below.
I thought about you far away in the countryside.
Will you visit us one day?
Will you write to me?

Good night,

Ruby

Dear Ruby,

Thank you for your letter. It is so cold today that I read it by the fire.

There's a lot of squawking going on outside. A big family of magpies lives in the hollow tree by my window. I'll tell you a secret – I can peep right inside their nest.

Do you know the Magpie Song? I've written it down just for you.

This is the song I sang to your daddy when he was a little boy.

I think about you every day, high in our apartment. I'd like to visit one day.

Send my love to everyone.

Grampa

THE MAGPIE SONG
(for my Ruby in the city)
1 for Sorrow,
2 for Joy,
3 for a Girl,
4 for a Boy,
5 for Silver,
6 for Gold,
7 for a Secret
never to be told.

Dear Grampa,

It's been cold here too. Mum and I got freezing waiting for the bus.

The lift isn't working and we had to carry the shopping up all 574 steps.

When we got in, Dad had already gone to work.

Did it snow where you are?

Are there wild animals in the woods?

Love from

Ruby

My dearest Ruby,

The woods are magical when it snows –
as white as the pages of a book. It tells you
the whole story of the night before if you know
how to read it. The words are animal footprints.

These marks are from a fox out hunting:

and these are where some deer
have crossed the lawn:

and these are the marks of those naughty old
magpies taking all the food from my bird table:

There were three magpies this morning –
3 for a girl. That's why I thought of you.

With fondest love,

Grampa.

Dear Grampa,

Dad says there are foxes in the city too. They live under the railway bridge. He says you see all kinds of secret things when you work nights.

Some people sleep down there because they don't have anywhere else to go.

I asked Dad about the Magpie Song but he said he didn't remember. He says he will make me a bird table for the balcony.

Please come and see me soon.

Love and kisses,

from

Ruby

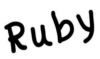

Dear Grampa,

Why haven't you written?

It's your turn to write.

Ruby

XXXXX

Dearest Ruby,

I'm sorry, I wasn't well. I slept for a long time.
Guess what woke me? The magpie family were fighting
by the hollow tree. There were so many I could hardly
count. Seven, I think - 7 for a secret.
They collect all kinds of shiny things
and hide them in their nests.
Here's a shiny secret for you to hide away,
Ruby, my magpie girl:

TOP SECRET

For Ruby only

I'm all right. Don't worry.

Grampa

P.S. I'm making a magpie necklace
for you. When it's finished,
I'll send it.

Dear Grampa,

I'm sorry you weren't well. We've got a secret too – a BIG secret! Guess what? Mum's going to have a baby. I was so happy, I ran on to the balcony and shouted, **"I'M GOING TO BE A SISTER!"**

Dad says he's happy too – except he doesn't know where the money will come from. Babies are expensive he says. Yesterday he took me to the park and we talked about the baby.

I like your secret. But PLEASE look after yourself. (I mean it!)

With love from **Ruby**

(Big Sister!!)

My dear Ruby,

Yes, I heard about the baby and I'm so pleased.
It will be born at Christmas, like a lovely present for
us all. Oh, I wish you could all come and live with me.
There's plenty of room, but you know there's no work here
for your dad. You'll have to wait a little while for
my visit Ruby, because I'm still not quite well.
Anyway, I've had plenty of time to finish your
little magpie necklace. It's made from a branch that fell
from the magpie tree. Now I'm going to paint it –
not just black and white. Magpies have a green and blue
sheen when you look at them carefully. I'll send it soon.
Here's a great big Grampy kiss for you.

X

Dear Grampa,

Thank you for my necklace. I love it. I carry it everywhere.
I take it secretly wherever I go. It's my lucky magpie.
Dad has been home all week. He seems sad.
He says there are too many bills to pay.
I asked him about when he was a boy and he showed me a photo.
He had long black hair, didn't he? He said he used to run through
the woods like a wild animal. Do you remember?

Here is a drawing of the new bird table
Dad made for me. It's just like
a tiny house for all the bird people.
What is your house like?

Lots and lots of love, R.

P.S. Mum says
the baby
can share
my room.

My dearest Ruby,

I'm writing this in bed because I've been poorly.
Yes, your daddy had long black hair and he rushed about
as free as a magpie. I taught him to carve wood
with a penknife, and now he can make anything.
My hair was black too but it's silver now, just like
the song: '5 for silver'.

This is what the house is like. It's an old secret
house in the side of the hill. It's got lots of windows
that need painting and the roof is wobbly. There are big
oak trees all around and that's where those old
magpies live. When I see them up there, I think about you
on your balcony above the city.

I wish you could fly away to me.

With all my love, from grumpy old Grampa

(stuck in bed).

Grampa,

Now the whole summer has gone and still you haven't been. I hope you're not poorly still? Have you been eating?

Yesterday a horrible letter came. It said they might take our apartment away if we don't pay more money. Mum and Dad were whispering all night — it's *their* secret and they don't want me to know, but I'm scared for the new baby. Will we all live under the railway?

The birds have been coming to the table, but there isn't much food.

Please write soon, because I really want you to.

Love,

Ruby

Dear Grampa,

Why don't you write? You promised to come.

Ruby

Ruby, my sweet, sweet girl.

There were four magpies this morning and I knew your brother was born.

The doctor won't let me write any more now but this is important, Ruby.

DON'T FORGET OUR SECRET!

And don't forget that I love you,

Grampa

Dear Baby,

Welcome to the world.

With love from
Ruby x x x

Grampa,

Something happened. I woke early because my brother was crying. I looked out on to the balcony and there was a big bird there. It looked like a magpie but magpies don't live in the city. He called to me.

He seemed hungry. Perhaps he'd flown a long way. Perhaps he'd forgotten to eat.

Then I remembered the song — 1 for sorrow.

Grampa, I'm sad.

You promised to come. Did you send the magpie instead?

Love

Ruby   X

Dear Grampa,

I don't know why I'm writing — just habit I suppose.

We love the house. Dad mended the roof and painted the windows. He put the bird table in the garden. He spends a lot of time doing wood carving now. This morning I heard him singing the Magpie Song.

I am 7 now, but when I run with my brother through the woods, I sometimes feel you are here.

I'll never forget you,

Ruby

Dear Ruby,

If you're reading this letter, you've found the secret! I knew you would. No one else would peep into the magpie tree.

Show the box to your father.

I carved six magpies on the lid.

You know why.

Be happy,

Grampa

Dear Grampa,

There were two magpies on the tree.

Thank you.

Ruby XXX

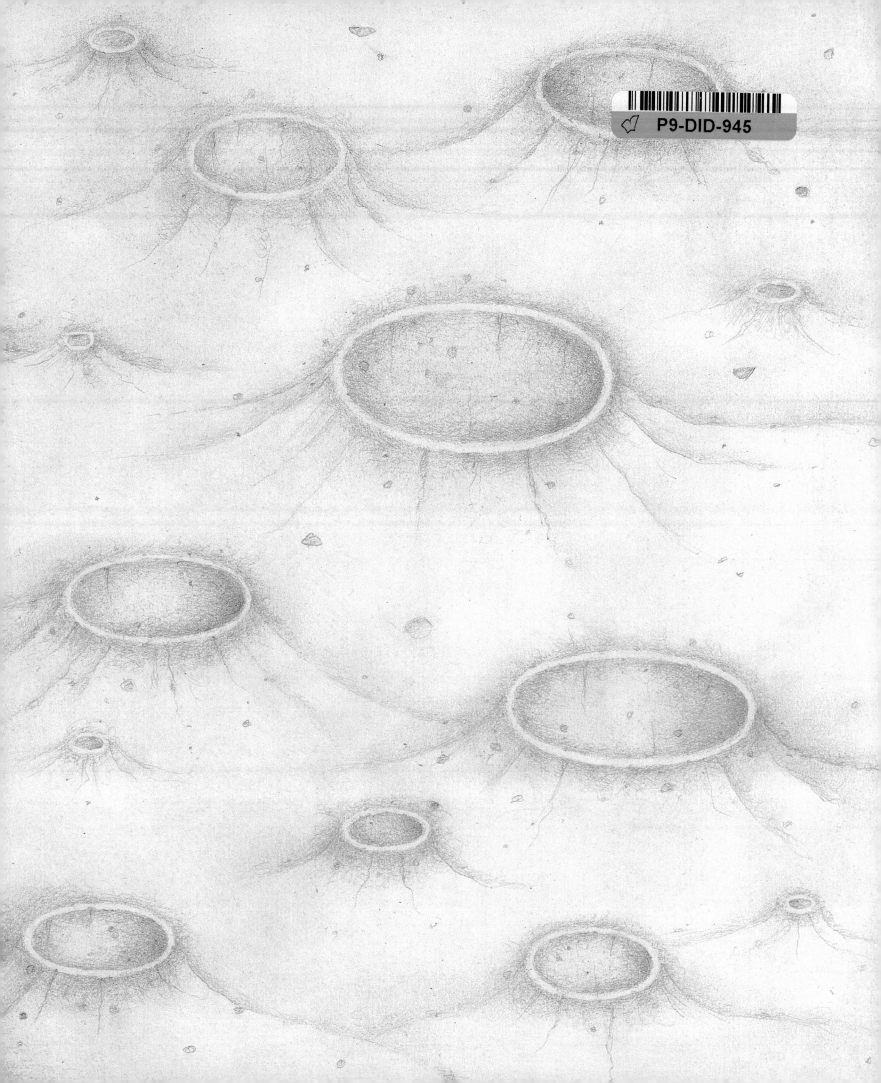

For Blue, an Earth dog—Helen
For Rosy, Phill, and Benny the dog—Wayne

Text copyright © 2005 by Helen Ward
Illustrations copyright © 2005 by Wayne Anderson

CIP Data is available.

Published in the United States 2007 by Dutton Children's Books,
a division of Penguin Young Readers Group
345 Hudson Street, New York, New York 10014
www.penguin.com/youngreaders

Originally published as Moon Dog in Great Britain 2005 by Templar Publishing,
an imprint of The Templar Company plc,
Pippbrook Mill, London Road, Dorking, Surrey, RH4 1JE, Great Britain
www.templarco.co.uk

Designed by Mike Jolley
Edited by A. J. Wood

Printed in Hong Kong

First American Edition

ISBN 0-525-47727-6

2 4 6 8 10 9 7 5 3 1

Little
MOON
DOG

by HELEN WARD illustrated by WAYNE ANDERSON

Dutton Children's Books

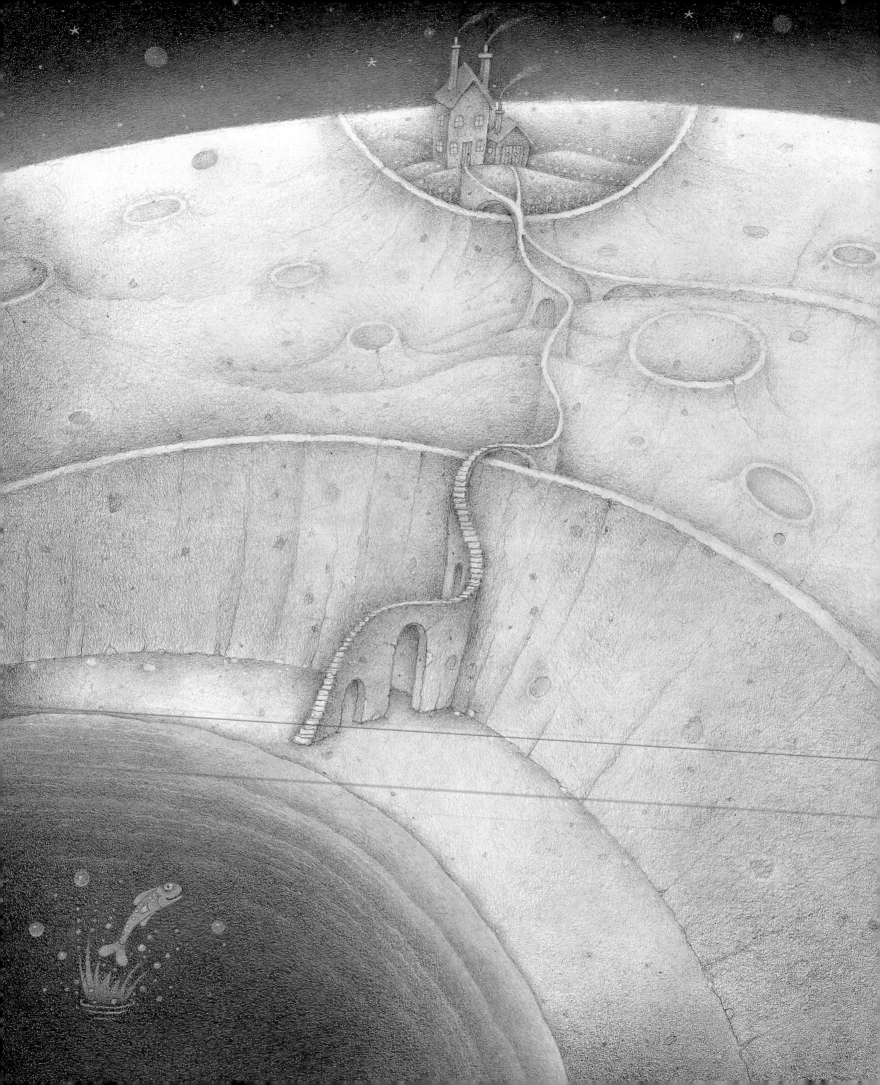

THE MOON IS USUALLY A PEACEFUL PLACE,

but once a year the gentle quiet is shattered by the arrival of . . .

. . . the RATTLING, clattering, clunkering, CLANKERING

of a tourist bus.

Like bad weather after thunder, strange summer visitors arrive.

They bring their buckets and spades to the tranquil beaches

and seven shades of trouble to the silvery gardens. . . .

THE MAN IN THE MOON knew

the mischievous tourists were up to no good.

Each year, as soon as they arrived, he locked his

front door and nailed his mailbox shut. Then he settled

into his comfortable armchair among his favorite books.

With Little Moon Dog curled happily at his feet,

the Man in the Moon waited for the noisy visitors

to go away.

BUT LITTLE MOON DOG

soon grew tired of sitting inside.

The strange visitors filled him with curiosity.

He watched as they poked holes in the rhumoonbarb

and unwound the moonbeans from their canes.

The tourists pulled silly faces at Little Moon Dog

through the window and called him out to play.

A S THE MAN IN THE MOON

dozed in his chair, Little Moon Dog

slipped out the back door and

into STRANGE company.

The visitors ruffled his ears and tickled his chin.

They cuddled Little Moon Dog and fed him sweet things.

His new friends even gave the little dog his own pair of wings.

They LAUGHED when he bounced and flapped and

tumbled after the sticks they threw for him.

WHEN THE MAN IN THE MOON called him

in for supper, Little Moon Dog didn't answer.

He was too busy playing to notice.

His new friends were wonderful! They taught him

to pinch plums and drop them down the chimney,

and to chase moonmoths across the starry sky

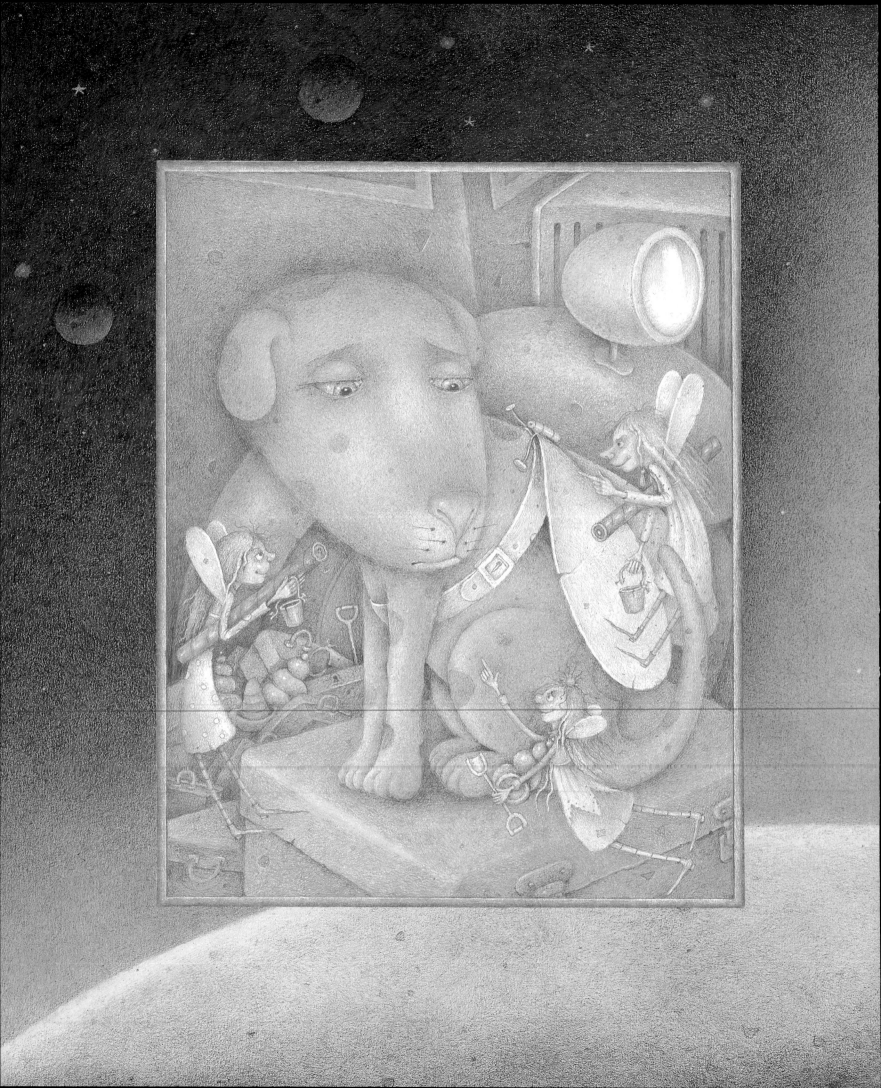

SOON it was time for the visitors to leave.

Little Moon Dog's flappety wings drooped sadly as they boarded the bus. He would miss his new friends.

Suddenly, they picked him up and packed him in among the sticky moon candy.

The little dog was so excited that he almost forgot about his old home, where the Man in the Moon dozed among well-read books. Moon Dog buried all thoughts of the Man in the Moon in the back of his head. He was so in love with his NEW friends that he wagged his tail ALL the way back through the moonlit night.

THE NEXT DAY, THE MAN IN THE MOON

looked for Little Moon Dog. He looked on every shelf.

He searched every cupboard, box, and basket.

He wandered through the tangled garden and among

the sandcastles on the silvery beaches.

He called and CALLED, but soon the Man

in the Moon realized that his Little Moon Dog . . .

. . . was FAR TOO FAR away to hear.

IN THE SHADY WOODS of a nearby planet, Little Moon Dog chased and fetched all the sticks that his new friends would throw. He learned all the tricks that they could teach. Then one day his friends decided they had better things to do than spend time with a silly Moon Dog.

They were bungling the flights of summer swallows

and swapping around seeds to unsettle the spring.

Little Moon Dog wanted to play with them, but his friends

were too busy making TROUBLE. They called him

Little Dog Stinker and shooed him away.

H

E SAT ALL ALONE among the high branches

as his friends played games with NEW creatures.

They tricked and teased, pinched and poked,

and forgot all about Little Moon Dog.

He realized that they weren't REALLY his friends at all.

Little Moon Dog suddenly felt very, VERY, VERY lonely.

He wished the Man in the Moon was there to comfort him.

He wished more than anything that he could

go HOME.

THE MAN IN THE MOON was lonely, too.

He thought of Little Moon Dog as he tidied the gardens

and mended all that had been broken by the rowdy visitors.

The moon was very quiet. TOO quiet.

The Man in the Moon missed his friend.

And so he made a plan. He took his toolbox from among

the cobwebs, brushed the moondust off an old garage door,

and turned a key in a rusty lock.

Later that night, a dark shadow rippled over the golden moon.

The Man in the Moon was leaving his home and starting out

on an adventure, for it was TIME to FIND his friend.

THE MAN FROM THE MOON searched

everywhere for Little Moon Dog.

By the time he reached the shady woods, he was

beginning to give up hope.

One cold evening he watched as the moon rose and cast

a silvery light among the leaves. Just then, a sad, thin sound

echoed through the trees. It brought a smile to the face

of the Man from the Moon.

L

ITTLE MOON DOG's homesick howl called to his

old friend. When the little dog finally saw the Man from

the Moon, his cry became a happy WOOF.

They were SO PLEASED to see each other.

Little Moon Dog scampered and flapped about

until the Man from the Moon caught him

out of the air. He hugged the little dog,

wrapped him up in his

great warm coat . . .

. . . and took him HOME.

NOW, whenever the gentle quiet of the moon is broken

by strange summer visitors, Little Moon Dog

and his BEST friend go away on a vacation

of their OWN.

F OR the Man in the Moon AND Little Moon Dog

know . . .

there is nothing quite so NASTY as a fickle FAIRY

and nothing quite so NICE as a faithful FRIEND.

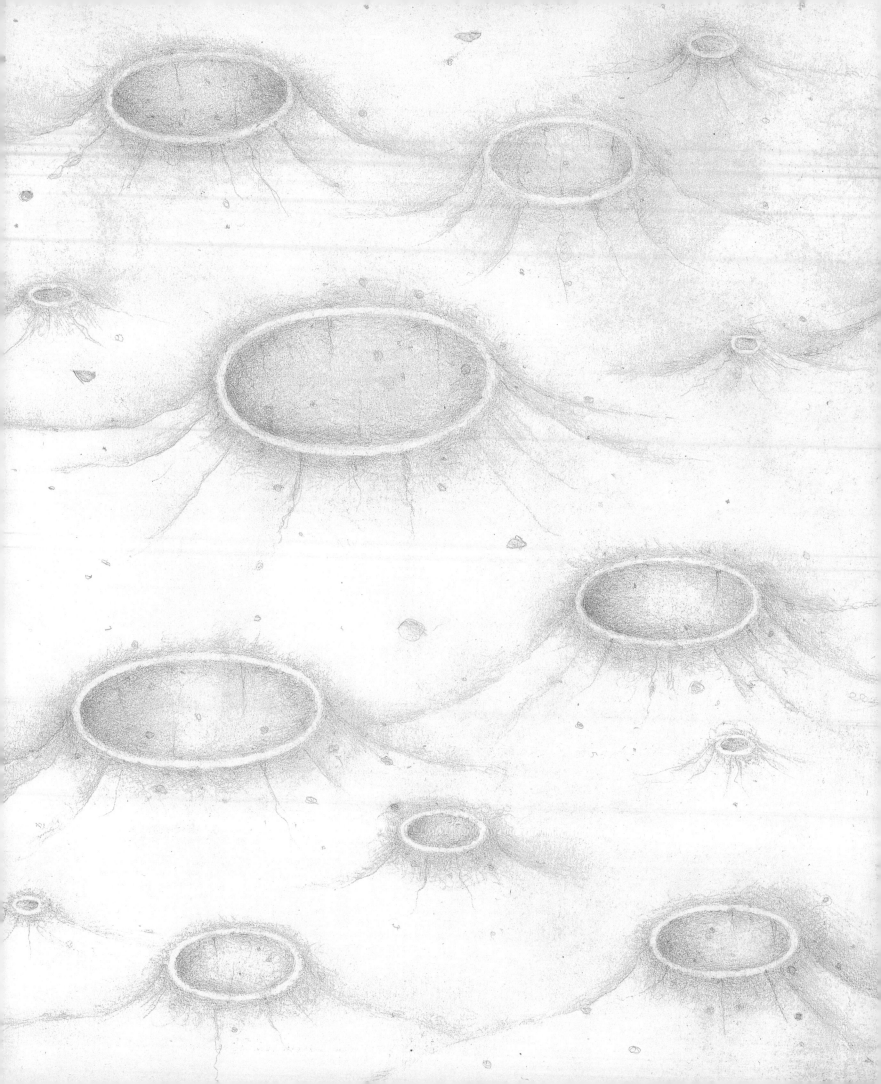

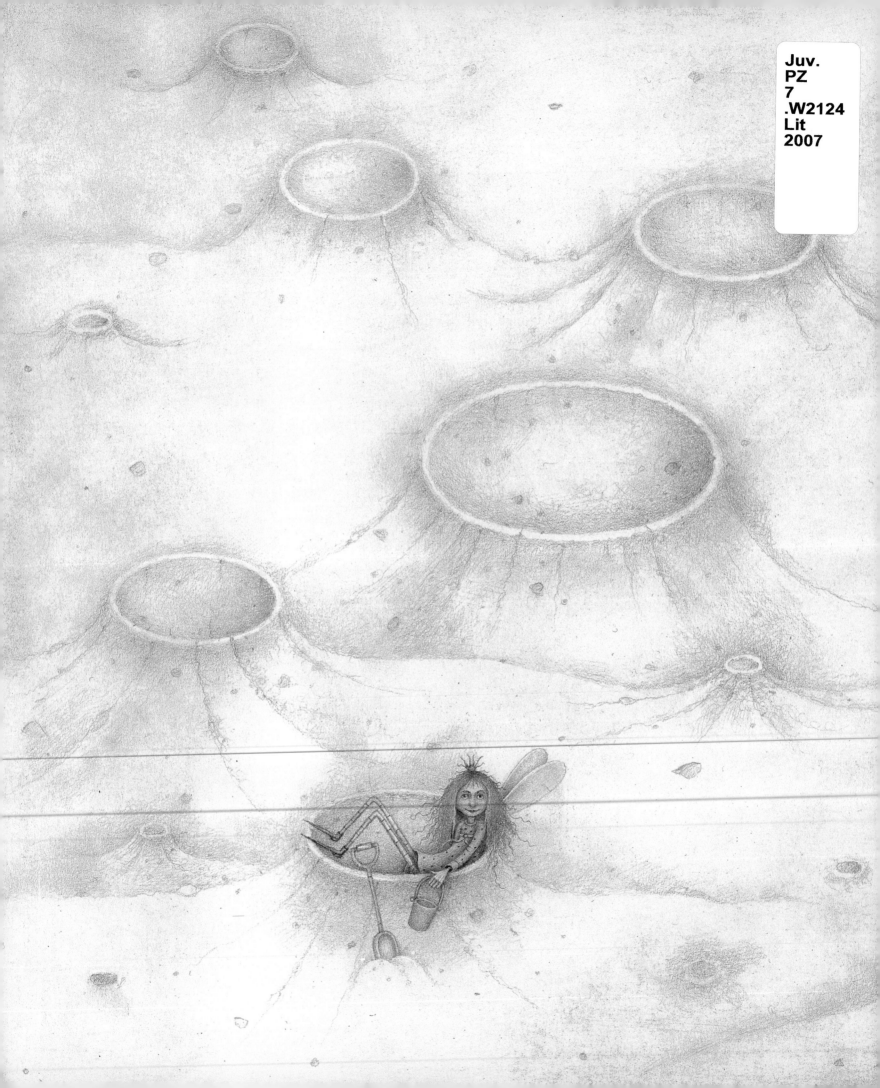